W9-AUA-702

THE
GLASS
MOUNTAIN

and Other Arabian Tales

By the author of

JACK   TAR

THE
GLASS
MOUNTAIN
and Other Arabian Tales

Written by
JEAN RUSSELL LARSON

Illustrated by
DONALD E. COOKE

MACRAE SMITH COMPANY · *Philadelphia*

C. 2

Library of Congress Catalog Card Number—71-38918

Trade ISBN 0-8255-5190-0
Library ISBN 0-8255-5191-9

Manufactured in the United States of America
Published simultaneously in Canada by George J. McLeod, Limited, Toronto

Contents

THE
GLASS
MOUNTAIN

IN former times, when demons, who have since withdrawn behind the veil of mystery, walked in the world openly, a wealthy merchant had a daughter whose name was Lalla. The time came when Lalla was old enough to marry and leave the merchant's house, but upon the subject of a suitable husband the young woman and her father could not agree.

Among the young men who traveled to the home of the merchant were princes and caliphs. But despite the magnificence of many of her suitors, Lalla was determined to wed a trader from Damascus. The merchant pleaded with his daughter for long days and nights, pointing out the wealth and position of other men, but

1

nothing would shake Lalla's resolve. At length the merchant hit upon what he believed to be a clever plan to gain his desires.

"Perhaps," he told his daughter, "I have overlooked the true worth of the trader Nuri. He must be a remarkable young man, since he has won your favor. Bring him to me tomorrow morning so that I may become better acquainted with him.

Lalla went away, rejoicing at her father's fairness.

On the following morning, Nuri presented himself before the merchant.

"It has come to my attention," the merchant said, "that my daughter has selected you from among all of the suitors who have come here, to be her husband. What do you believe to be the reason for her choice, since you have neither wealth nor high station in life?"

"I am honest," Nuri offered, "and not entirely without brains. As a matter of fact, I am rather clever."

"I am pleased to hear that," the merchant replied smoothly. "I could not permit my daughter to marry a fool. But since I have not seen evidence of your cleverness, perhaps you would not object to proving it to me."

"What proof would you require?" Nuri asked suspiciously.

The merchant closed his eyes and leaned back in his chair, seeming to consider the matter for some minutes.

"In the garden of this house," he said, at length, "there are buried three pots of gold."

"That fact must afford you much happiness," Nuri said.

"Not so," the merchant replied, "for the pots are guarded by a terrible ogre. Not only is the ogre fierce, but he is also exceedingly cunning, and I fear my pots of gold may never be rescued from his clutches."

The merchant sighed as if in great despair.

"Fear not," Nuri cried. "I shall this day liberate the gold from the hands of the ogre."

"Are you not afraid?" the merchant asked.

"Of course I am not afraid!" Nuri scoffed. "It will be the simplest thing in the world for me to separate the ogre from the gold."

Then the merchant declared that if Nuri succeeded in his mission, he would be awarded the hand of Lalla in marriage. But if he failed, then he must agree to go away from the merchant's house at once.

Nuri was directed to the garden, an oasis of green set thickly with roses and dotted with sparkling fountains.

"Now I shall commence my work," Nuri said. "The first step is to become acquainted with the ogre."

He set out across the garden.

"Ogre," he called, cupping his hands about his mouth, "please show yourself."

In only a moment there rose from the thicket a large and fierce-looking creature.

"I am Ox-Foot," he roared, "son of the king of the nether world. Who are you, and why do you seek me?"

"I am Nuri, trader from Damascus," Nuri told him. "I wish to marry the daughter of the merchant in whose garden you dwell."

"What is that to me?" Ox-Foot demanded.

Nuri sat down on the grass beside Ox-Foot. "The situation is as follows," he began. "The merchant, having the best interests of his daughter at heart, wishes evidence that I am a worthy suitor. Since I have neither wealth nor high position, I must prove myself clever. The merchant has set as a task for me the rescuing of three pots filled with gold which lie buried in this garden and which, I understand, you guard."

"What a pity success will not crown your efforts," the ogre said. "You will not be as fortunate in this endeavor as was a young man of Baghdad who sometime since rode a donkey to the summit of the mountain of glass, thereby winning a princess."

"I am not familiar with that story," Nuri said with interest.

"Then I will tell it to you," Ox-Foot replied, settling himself comfortably on the grass.

The Glass Mountain

ONCE upon a time, a certain Mirza from the land of the lion and the sun declared his desire to wed the daughter of the Sultan of India.

"You shall marry the Princess Zara," the sultan said, "upon the day when you recover a casket of jewels which has been stolen from me by a wicked djinn and spirited away to the top of the mountain of glass."

You must know that many men had attempted to recover those jewels and all of them had failed.

"I shall proceed at once to accomplish the deed," Mirza announced.

He went home immediately and took as provisions for the journey forty dates, which he put in his pockets. Then he took up his journey and went and went without stopping until he reached a city situated at the foot of the glass mountain.

Having eaten all of his dates and being very hungry, Mirza looked about for a likely source of food. His glance alighted upon a market stall where an old woman sat amid a pile of fruit.

"Pay attention, old woman," he said, addressing her. "I am in need of provisions to carry with me up the side of the glass mountain."

"I will give you good advice," the old woman replied. "Do not go. But if you must go, then take as your companion a donkey, leaving here with me the horse you are now riding."

"I shall do as I please," Mirza replied smartly.

As these things were going on, a merchant stood by, listening. "The old woman advises you wisely," he said. "No fewer than twenty horsemen have attempted to gain the summit of Glass Mountain. All have failed and slipped to their doom."

"I have considered the matter," Mirza announced, "and I have decided to ride upon a donkey, leaving my horse here. It now remains for me to locate the exact donkey for my purpose."

"In that endeavor I am able to assist you," the merchant said.

"You will do me a great favor," Mirza told him.

The merchant left them and returned minutes later with a small donkey wearing crimson slippers on his forefeet.

DON

"How do you come to possess such charming footwear?" Mirza inquired of the donkey.

"More about that later, my dear," the donkey replied.

The mare was exchanged for the donkey, and Mirza, carrying a melon under his arm, commenced his journey up the side of the mountain.

"May good luck attend you," the merchant and the old woman called together, as Mirza began his ascent.

At midday, as was his custom, Mirza halted to eat. Having cut the melon, he offered a generous portion of it to the donkey, who accepted it gratefully.

"Pray tell me, now," Mirza requested, "the story of the crimson slippers, since I have never before seen a donkey with such fine apparel."

"O excellent master," the donkey began, "I was born in the city of Fas. Now you must know that all in my family were shoemakers. My father and mother were shoemakers, and so were all my cousins. We dwelled there happily until one day a monster came against the city.

" 'I have come to eat up all of the shoemakers!' the monster cried, raging at the gates. 'A shoemaker has done me injury, and I will not rest until I have gained revenge!'

"Upon examination, it was learned that a certain wicked shoemaker of Smyrna had fashioned for the monster a pair of ill-fitting shoes that pinched and pained at each step. In vain did my family plead to be allowed to make up for the crime, offering to provide the grandest and best-fitting of footwear. The monster declared he must simply devour each shoemaker in his path, and there was no help for it."

"How did you escape such a terrible fate?" Mirza asked with great interest. "For since I see you here, I am certain that you did escape."

"Indeed I did escape, oh worthy master," the donkey said. "I alone, of all my family, eluded the monster. I achieved this by concealing myself in a flock of sheep, covering myself with a woolly hide and bleating in tune with those around me. Then I slipped through the gate while the monster took his ease, carrying with me only the slippers you see upon my feet as a token of my former occupation. From that day, I have been in the employ of the merchant you met below and the old woman who is clever beyond measure."

Mirza's eyes grew wide with interest.

"How many tricks has she?" he asked.

"That is unknown to me," the donkey admitted. "She plans many treacheries in company with the merchant, and her purpose in helping you is an evil one."

"Please advise me of her intentions," Mirza begged.

"It is her plan," the donkey said, "to relieve you of the sultan's jewels. A horse cannot gain the summit of Glass Mountain, but never before has the old woman been able to persuade a fortune hunter to exchange a horse for a donkey. You have fallen into her trap."

"I will prove a match for her cunning!" Mirza cried.
"In the meantime, I am glad to have taken advantage
of your services, since I will be successful in climbing
the mountain, which is after all the first step."

The side of the mountain was very slippery, and
even the donkey found the climb a difficult one. Mirza
clung to the animal's back without complaint.

Now Mirza and the donkey saw the tracks of the
jewel-thieving djinn, and each track was two feet wide.
They followed the tracks on and on and on, until they
came to the lair of the djinn at the very peak of the
slippery mountain. The light of the dying sun shone red
upon the glass, nearly blinding Mirza.

"In that lair," he said to the donkey, "must dwell the
evil djinn. I shall enter immediately and recover the
jewels of the sultan."

Whereupon the djinn, who had been listening to
Mirza's words, jumped fiercely out of his lair.

"Greetings to you!" he roared. "I regret the necessity
of eating you up."

"Such tender feelings do credit to you," Mirza
replied, bowing deeply. "Perhaps there is some way
out of the situation."

"Let us discuss the matter over an evening meal,"
the djinn suggested, eyeing the remaining melon
Mirza carried. "It has been some time since I tasted
fresh fruit, and I prefer it to all other food, particularly
Persians and donkeys."

They sat together, sharing the melon, while the sun sank behind the mountain and the first stars shone in the night sky.

"I have spent my time," the djinn told Mirza, "amassing a great fortune. I possess not only the jewels of the Sultan of India, but other riches as well. But on this mountain, where the winds cross and the moon sleeps, sadness overtakes me."

"What is the reason for that?" Mirza inquired.

"I will tell you," the djinn replied.

"Formerly, I reigned as king of a city on the shore of the great salt sea. It is my belief that I ruled my subjects with justice and wisdom. One day a lion clad in an ermine cape came to the city. 'Such a splendid beast!' the people cried. 'We must proclaim him king.' That they did. A feast was held in his honor, drums beat, and trumpets sounded. I left the city rather than remain an ordinary citizen where once I had been king. Though I have become wealthy, I long to return home. It is written, 'The tar of my country is better than the honey of others.' "

"It is also written," Mirza said, 'The world has not promised anything to anybody.' If you would return to your home as king, then you had better be about it. Have you no way to impress the fickle people of the city, causing them to turn from the lion to you?"

The djinn sighed.

"I have thought a great deal about the matter," he said, "but earrings of gold or a satin turban would not impress my former subjects, since any man of wealth could acquire such items. I can think of nothing that would lend me sufficient elegance."

The donkey shifted his position, leaning close to the djinn.

"Slippers," he said.

"You will pardon my inattention," the djinn said. "For but a moment I thought you said 'slippers.' "

"Slippers," the donkey repeated.

"O," the djinn wailed, "I am indeed luck-forsaken. Now, in addition to all of my troubles, I am visited by a donkey who jibbers about footwear."

"I was only saying," the donkey explained patiently, "that you might acquire a splendorous pair of slippers, the like of which have never before been seen in your city, and thereby win the admiration of your former subjects."

"I hear your words," the djinn scoffed, "and I am reminded that it is written: 'Among walnuts, only the empty one speaks.' "

"I take no offense at your remarks," the donkey said, "for it is also written: 'People do not throw stones at trees which have no fruit.' I only ask you to lean close and examine the slippers I wear. You will find them to be of rare quality and to possess a particular magic which is no longer found in the world, since my entire family, blessings upon them, were devoured by an especially offensive monster."

"You did not tell me that the slippers were magical," Mirza complained.

"You did not ask me," the donkey replied. "And it is not my custom to travel the countryside crying aloud all that I know. If your brains did not hang at the top of your turban, you would have guessed that no ordinary family of donkeys could earn bread by shoemaking."

The djinn leaned close to the donkey and examined, by the light of the moon, the crimson slippers the donkey wore.

"I am no stranger to magic," the djinn remarked, "and I sense there is power in these slippers. What magic is it, and what price would you require for the slippers?"

The donkey seemed to consider for several minutes.

"Two things I would require," he said at last. "First, that you give into Mirza's possession the casket of jewels which rightfully belongs to the Sultan of India; second, that Mirza agree to take me along with him, in the event we are able to escape the clutches of the merchant and the old woman at the foot of the mountain, and make a home for me where I may resume my career as a shoemaker."

"My part of the bargain is as good as done!" the djinn cried, jumping to his feet and disappearing into his lair. In but a moment he returned, carrying a casket that spilled over with rubies and strings of pearls.

"As for my part of the bargain," Mirza said, "I am in your hands entirely. If we are able to elude the merchant and the old woman, you may be sure of a home with me."

"Two things remain to be settled," the djinn said,

turning to the donkey. "You have not as yet disclosed the nature of the magic attendant upon the slippers, and you have not explained how I can wear them. Perhaps your plan is that I shall hang them from my ears, since they are so small in size and I am so large."

The donkey smiled, and neither Mirza nor the djinn was at all astonished, since you may be sure that in a day when donkeys spoke they also smiled.

"Both matters may be taken care of at the same time," the donkey said, "for the magic the slippers possess allows them to be increased or decreased in size at will, as well as many other amazing things, among which are the following: While wearing the slippers you may perceive a lie when it is spoken, know the key to opening all hearts, and fly as a bird flies."

Whereupon the djinn took the slippers from the hands of the donkey, put them on his feet, and went up into the sky.

"This is most remarkable," Nuri said, when the ogre reached that point in the story.

"More about the djinn another time," the ogre said. "Now I will relate to you the story of how Mirza and the donkey escaped capture by the merchant and the old woman," and he continued his tale:

Having gained possession of the casket of jewels

and bidden farewell to the djinn, who was sailing majestically through the night sky, Mirza and the donkey settled down to sleep.

Next morning, when the glass mountain was bathed in sunlight, Mirza took the casket of jewels under his arm, mounted the donkey, and began the descent down the mountain.

"It occurs to me," he said to the donkey, "that with the help of the slippers you could have caused us to fly to the top of the mountain yesterday. Did such a thought occur to you?"

"I sought to test you," the donkey replied. "Since I hoped that circumstances might make you my permanent master, I wished to learn the extent of your courage and daring. I was pleased to find that you did not complain when the way was difficult and treacherous. I trust you will continue to behave yourself in that fashion and that I will never have cause to reproach you."

Mirza gave his word and clung tightly to the neck of the donkey as it inched down the glass slope.

When they came in sight of the foot of the mountain, Mirza saw the merchant and the old woman, standing together and craning their necks to see whether or not the jewels had come down in the company of the young man.

"Greetings, you on the back of the donkey!" the old woman called. "We have sent up many prayers for your safe return."

"I am grateful to you," Mirza replied. "You shall not go unrewarded."

"True!" the merchant and the old woman muttered together.

The donkey reached the foot of the mountain and halted.

"You see before you," Mirza announced, "the casket of jewels which I redeemed from the djinn by overcoming him. The wicked creature has gone away and in all likelihood will never return."

"We see the jewels," the merchant and the old woman chorused happily.

"If I were a selfish man," Mirza said with a smile of charity, "I would toss a few of these baubles to you in thanks for your advice and the loan of your donkey and be on my way. But I will not do that."

"You won't?" the old woman croaked.

Mirza lounged against the stall and plucked a few grapes from a bunch, dropping them daintily into his upturned mouth.

"Oh no!" he assured her.

"See here," the old woman began, "if you do not at once hand over to us that casket of jewels, we will be forced——"

"Now," Mirza cried, "you have come to the heart of the matter! Do you think it has escaped my attention that you, an old woman, are forced by circumstances to earn a living by peddling fruit in the dusty street? Oh no! I saw at once your plight and my heart went out to you.

"And you," he continued, turning to the merchant, "are little better situated. Fortune has brought me here, I am convinced of it! In addition to retrieving the jewels that will gain me a bride, I will be able to rescue you two from desperate circumstances."

The merchant and the old woman stared at Mirza.

"You see," Mirza confided, dropping his voice to a whisper, "I have discovered that the djinn was an exceedingly successful thief who stole not only these jewels but, in addition, a great quantity of gold, ivory, and ostrich feathers."

"Ostrich feathers?" the old woman cried with delight. "Are you certain about that?"

"Would I, who am so grateful to you, tell an untruth?" Mirza asked in a tone of injured pride. "But all of the djinn's booty lies at the top of the mountain. You must go there before the wind whispers this secret to other ears. I advise you to leave at once."

The merchant and the old woman danced about in the street, squealing aloud in anticipation of the riches that would be theirs.

"We will need the donkey," the merchant said suddenly. "Please climb down from his back so that we may mount and commence our journey."

The donkey shrank back in horror.

"You promised," he hissed to Mirza, "that I would go away with you."

Mirza put on a sad face.

"If only I could give you this donkey . . ." he said mournfully.

"You can!" the old woman snapped. "It is easy."

Mirza shook his head. "Before I was able to overcome him, the djinn, wicked creature that he was, cast a spell on this unfortunate beast. The donkey has but moments to live, and I have given my word that he shall view the onion garden at the outskirts of the city before he dies. You would not deny him that one request."

The old woman wiped a tear from her eye.

"Go," she cried bountifully. "We will find another donkey."

The merchant and the old woman went away, talking excitedly. But Mirza and the donkey set out for India, where Mirza delivered the jewels into the hands of the sultan and wed the Princess Zara.

As for the donkey, he immediately resumed his career as a shoemaker, serving all who appreciated the finest in apparel. He lived long and was the father of a large family whose members still fashion shoes, but they have withdrawn into the realm of magic.

"That is a very interesting history," Nuri said, when the ogre had finished. My thanks to you for telling it to me. I would like to achieve success in my venture as did Mirza in his."

"You and I are not in the same positions as were Mirza and the djinn," the ogre told him. "There is nothing you possess that would benefit me in the slightest; therefore we cannot make an exchange of goods."

Nuri thought about that.

"What you say is true," he admitted, "but matters of this kind have often been settled by other means. I am reminded of a story."

"Tell it to me," the ogre suggested.

Ali and the Griffin

ONCE a young man of Samarkand went to study with the taleb Sidi Mahomet Soliman. There he studied law and was a model pupil. One night a griffin came and carried off the young man, whose name was Ali, to an island in the sea.

"This is good enough for you!" the griffin said, and left him there.

Ali pondered long upon the words of the griffin and what they might mean, for he was a scholar, as I have told you, and accustomed to giving matters great thought. At any rate, no action was open to him, since he was entirely surrounded by water and possessed no boat.

After many days and nights spent in thought, Ali

decided that the griffin had probably mistaken him for another and less worthy young man, who deserved punishment. He decided to go in search of the griffin, explain the mistake to him, and return to his studies. Whereupon he cast about for some means of fashioning a boat, the better to escape from the island.

At length Ali gathered together all manner of boughs and vines and set about making the boat, which in nearly no time was completed. Then the scholar set out, using the stars as his guide.

In twenty days' time, just as the store of dates which he had taken from the island as provisions was at an end, Ali reached shore. As fortune would have it, the griffin was on hand to greet him.

"I see you have come," the griffin said.

"It would appear so," Ali replied.

The griffin sighed. "Patience is the key of joy," he said.

He took Ali up and went and went with him until they reached the very heart of the sand country, which is a desolate region with neither shade nor water.

"Try and behave yourself," the griffin said. He dropped him there and went away.

Ali watched him leave and sat down to think the matter through. "If only he had allowed me to explain about the mistaken identity!" Ali thought. "But there is no remedy for what has happened." Then he set out across the sand, traveling by night and sleeping during the hours of sunlight.

After many days and nights, Ali arrived, closer to death than life, in a town on the edge of the desert. There he found the griffin.

"There is no news in the world which has not been heard," the griffin said when he saw Ali.

"I have come to explain something to you," Ali replied. "I am a scholar and have, each day of my life, paid heed only to my own business. Therefore I conclude that the punishment you have meted out to me was meant for another, more troublesome, fellow."

"Punishment?" the griffin screeched, staring at Ali. "Do you call it punishment to rescue you from the very jaws of death? For that is exactly what I have been attempting to do."

"Kindly tell me about it," Ali requested politely, seating himself at the griffin's feet. "I cannot help but believe you have made a mistake."

The griffin settled down beside Ali, folding his wings neatly.

"It has come to my attention," the griffin began, "that you became heir to a sizable fortune upon the death of your father. It has further reached my ears that your uncle, a wicked and greedy man, is at this very moment on his way from the city of Istanbul with the intent to deprive you of that money."

"I will be happy to share my fortune with my uncle!" Ali cried.

"Ah," the griffin said, raising a paw to silence Ali, "I did not say that your uncle wishes a share of the money. He intends to have all of it. You must realize that as your next of kin he will gain the entire fortune upon the occasion of your death."

Ali breathed a sigh of relief. "Then I have no worry," he said, "for I am in the best of health."

The griffin groaned. "For a scholar," he said, "you are dull-witted. Your uncle's intention is to hasten your death, thereby gaining the money for himself. Now you understand why I have taken an interest in your case, and why I have attempted, vainly it seems, to keep you from harm's way."

"I understand," Ali said thoughtfully, "and I am grateful to you. But I cannot remain hidden from my uncle forever. The time will come when we must meet and settle this matter."

The griffin thought about that.

"You are right," he said at length, sighing. "One must face unpleasantness. It is written: 'The world is a seven-headed serpent which gives not one moment's rest to anyone.'"

"It is also written," Ali replied, "that cotton and fire play not together. I fear I shall be no match for my uncle."

"Do not trouble yourself," the griffin said. "I am on your side, and I have a plan."

"Griffins often do," Ali replied. "Pray tell it to me."

"You must convince your uncle," the griffin said, "that money brings with it more trouble than joy. In that way, you will also persuade him to go away and leave you in peace."

Ali stared at the griffin.

"The possession of a large amount of money is often a troublesome thing," he said, "but how will I go about convincing my uncle of that fact before he has killed me and taken my fortune for himself?"

"That is your problem," the griffin snapped, "and no concern of mine. But since I have taken an interest in your situation, please advise me of the outcome. I shall remain here while you go to confront your uncle—who will, I judge, arrive in the city tomorrow. May fortune smile upon your efforts. Goodbye."

Ali went away, struggling with the problem the griffin had presented him with. At length the troubled young man decided to leave his future in the hands of fate.

The following day dawned, as Ali had feared that it would.

Shortly after dawn, a knock sounded at the door of Ali's house. When Ali answered the summons he found on the doorstep a tall black-robed man whom he guessed at once to be his uncle.

"You have come," Ali said.

"It would appear so," his uncle replied, pushing past Ali and entering the house. "I am Gasim, brother of your late father and your only living relative. I have come in order that we may become better acquainted."

Ali made his uncle welcome, scurrying to order a meal prepared.

"You must be a prosperous young man," Gasim said slyly, when the meal was finished and the two had settled down in comfort. "To what do you attribute your wealth?"

"Bad fortune," Ali said morosely.

Gasim stared at him openmouthed.

"Bad fortune?" he echoed in surprise. "To be a wealthy man and to live in luxury is the result of good fortune. I fear that your wits have become unhinged."

"Oh," Ali cried, "you do not know what you are saying! But if you were to live one day as the possessor of wealth, you would know that I am correct in saying that the owner of riches is a star-crossed man."

"I accept your challenge!" Gasim cried spiritedly. "I shall commence at once."

"Have you a plan?" Ali asked.

"I have," Gasim replied. "I shall show you that wealth is joy."

Clapping his hands, Gasim summoned the cook. "I wish a feast prepared," he said, "since I intend to invite the most important men of the city to a banquet honoring me."

The cook eyed Gasim suspiciously, then looked at Ali, who nodded his head in affirmation.

"If I am to prepare a feast," the cook said, "I must have food from the market." She began ticking off the required items on her fingers. "I will need lamb and rice," she said, "and coffee and dates, and——"

"Go and secure the necessary items at once," Gasim cried bountifully. "Cost is no object."

The cook's eyes grew wide. "I?" she demanded. "I

will not go to the market. If I am to prepare a banquet, then I must have rest. I will take a nap while you go to the market."

She went away.

"A wealthy man should not be addressed in that manner," Gasim said. "Nor should he be forced to do the marketing. However, I am new at this game, so I will do what must be done."

He dressed himself in Ali's finest cloak, secured a bagful of gold coins from his nephew, and went to the market.

"Buy us some cakes, Baba!" a crowd of boys called to Gasim, as he entered the market.

"I have come to purchase provisions for my cook," Gasim replied. "I cannot afford to buy cakes for all of you."

"Untrue!" one of the boys shouted.

"False friend!" another shouted. "Shame!"

Gasim made his way to the stall of a fruit vendor, but the group of boys followed him, jeering.

"See the fine cloak!" one of the boys called. "See the bulging purse. Miser!"

The other boys took up the cry, until a crowd had gathered to see what the cause of such a disturbance could be.

"Buy cakes for them!" an old woman called.

"Buy cakes for them!" others echoed.

Gasim's face grew crimson. He opened his purse,

fumbling in his haste to place coins in the hands of the boys, thereby silencing them.

"Ah," the boys cried, when they had received the money. "You are a generous man! Kindly disregard all of the other things we formerly said about you."

"Go and buy your cakes," Gasim snapped, "and leave me in peace. I have business to attend to."

The crowd dispersed and Gasim approached the fruit vendor.

"I wish to purchase some dates," Gasim said.

"Certainly," the merchant cried heartily. "Only the finest for such a man as you."

He scooped up a handful of dates and thrust them at Gasim.

"Ten pieces of gold and these dates are yours," he said.

"Ten pieces of gold for a handful of common dates?" Gasim gasped. "You cannot be serious!"

"Of course I am serious," the merchant replied. "To begin with, these are not common dates but exquisite fruit, gathered at the peak of flavor from the topmost reaches of the palms by the gentlest and most reverent of workers. In addition to that fact, you are obviously a wealthy man and can pay a high price."

"Robber!" Gasim roared. "You are taking advantage of me."

"Yes," the merchant agreed thoughtfully, "I am. But you can afford it. Shall we do business?"

"Never!" Gasim bellowed.

He went away, but at each stall in the market his experience was the same. As soon as a merchant caught sight of Gasim's splendid cloak and fat purse, prices rose to great heights.

At last, tired and discouraged and empty-handed, Gasim made his way back to Ali's house.

"Where are the provisions for the banquet?" Ali asked.

"There will be no banquet," Gasim replied. He told his nephew what had happened at the market.

"What a pity!" Ali cooed, when the tale was finished. "Perhaps your next project will meet with more success. What is to be your next project?"

"I have decided," Gasim said, "to go to the place where the important men of the city gather and walk among them, allowing them to make my acquaintance."

Then he went to the center of the city and indeed found a group of respected citizens talking of this and that and cooling themselves in the shade of the bazaar.

"I have come to join your gathering," Gasim said. "Where would you like me to sit?"

"Who are you?" asked a tall, bearded man, as all heads turned to look at the newcomer.

"I am Gasim, and I am a very wealthy man," Gasim replied. "I have here a purse filled with gold coins."

"You are also a very boastful fellow," a small man

snapped. "What makes you think you are welcome here?"

"Why," Gasim cried, "I have money!"

The small man laughed sarcastically. "Money will not make you welcome here," he said. "We are men who work hard and play little. We come here to relax from our labors and discuss the business of the city. What work do you do?"

Gasim stared at him. "I do no work," he said.

"Then you must be a very dull fellow," the bearded man said. "We are poets, merchants, and craftsmen. We have no need of an idle rich man. Go where you will be appreciated."

Gasim went away, shaking his head. As he walked, he saw a man clad in a tattered cloak and torn sandals.

"Here, my poor fellow," Gasim cried importantly, "take this coin and purchase some decent clothing for yourself."

"What do you mean by that?" the man demanded. "Why have you accosted me in the street?"

"I only meant to be of some help to you," Gasim explained.

"I need no help from you!" the man shouted. He began waving his arms about in the air. "Who are you to call my clothing indecent? What gives you the right to insult me?"

A crowd gathered once again.

"This man has insulted me!" the fellow said, pointing a long finger at Gasim. "Because he has money he believes he can go about the streets injuring the pride of honest citizens!"

"Shame!" the crowd shouted.

Gasim tucked his purse into the folds of his cloak and hurried off down the street, anxious for the safety of Ali's house.

"Do you still wish to be a wealthy man?" Ali asked, when Gasim had told his story.

"I will be honest with you," Gasim replied. "I came here to relieve you of your entire fortune. I was prepared to use any means necessary in order to gain all of your wealth."

"But now you have seen the error of your ways," Ali guessed, "and you wish no money at all. Am I correct?"

"Not exactly," Gasim said. "Since I was your father's brother, I claim a share of your fortune. Please be good enough to hand it over, and be grateful that I am not taking all you have."

Ali did as he was bidden.

"What of the words of the important men of the city?" Ali asked his uncle. "Did they make no impression on you? Do you not wish to make some contribution to the world by doing honest work?"

"I may think about that," Gasim replied, and went away.

Ali hastened to the griffin and reported what had

happened, being glad to have escaped with his life and a portion of his inheritance.

"It is written," the griffin said, " 'Sacrifice your beard for your head.' You did as well as could have been expected in the exchange, and I am proud of you."

"Is it your plan," the ogre asked, when Nuri had finished the story, "to put your cause in the hands of fate, as Ali did, trusting that I will see reason and compromise with you?"

"That might happen," Nuri suggested. "Both Ali and his uncle were satisfied with the outcome of their situation."

"A clear-cut victory is always better," the ogre said firmly. "I am reminded of an incident in which a bird overcame a lion and a fox, thereby saving himself from certain death."

"Remarkable!" Nuri cried. "Please tell me about it."

The Lion,
the Fox and the Bird

ONCE a lion and a fox went to live in a certain forest. There dwelled in that forest a bird who was plump and slow of wing.

"You should leave this place at once," the bird was advised by his friends. "Go and seek shelter far from here, for the lion with his strength will overcome you and devour you; and if he does not, then the cunning fox will surely make a meal of you."

But the bird was not afraid. He said to his friends, "Where would I find another home so fine? I shall not leave. Instead I shall force the lion and the fox to go."

At this the bird's friends laughed and called him a foolish and boastful fellow.

Now the lion had seen the plump bird, and he said to the fox, "That bird will be a good mouthful."

"You will never taste it," the fox replied, "for I mean to eat it myself."

Whereupon the lion roared with anger and said, "You cannot match my strength. The bird will be mine!"

"You cannot match my wits," the fox replied. "The bird will be mine!"

And it happened, as the lion and the fox disputed among themselves, that the bird flew down from a tall tree and addressed them. "Oh, sirs," he said, "how happy I am that you have come here, for I am in need of food and can find none."

Now the lion and the fox were surprised to see the bird standing before them in this manner. The lion thought to pounce upon the bird, but it would be shameful to kill a creature who had come to ask for help.

"What can we do for you?" the fox asked.

The bird looked to the left.

"There are berries there, in the thicket," he said, "and my mouth waters for the taste of them, but I cannot reach the bushes."

"Why is that?" the lion asked.

"The bushes are caught beneath some fallen trees," the bird answered, "and I have not strength enough to free them."

"That is no problem," the lion said and straightaway

went among the trees, pushing them aside with his mighty paws until the berry bushes were uncovered.

The bird then feasted upon the berries until he had his fill, thanked the lion politely, and went on his way.

"Why did you help him?" the fox asked.

"What else could I do," the lion pleaded, "when he laid his problem at my very feet? He needed me."

On the following day, as the lion and the fox walked among the trees, the bird came again to them.

"How happy I am to see you!" he said. "I need your help once again."

"What is it this time?" the lion asked.

The bird looked to the right, where the wide river flowed. "There, in the river," he said, "are some tall reeds that would make a fine nest. But I am not suited by nature to enter the water and so I cannot gather the reeds."

"That is no problem," said the cunning fox. Whereupon he went forward to the river and addressed himself to a group of herons standing on the bank.

"Look how those reeds cloud the water," he said. "If the reeds were gone, you would see the juicy fish more clearly."

Seeing the wisdom of the fox's words, the herons made haste to pull up the reeds with their beaks and place them on the riverbank.

"There are your reeds," said the fox to the bird. "Now you may build your nest."

"Why did you help him?" the lion asked.

"I could do nothing else when he laid his problem at my very feet," the fox answered. "He needed me."

It was but a day later when the bird came again to the lion and the fox. "How happy I am to see you, sirs," he said, "for I must ask your help once again."

"What is it now?" growled the fox. How he longed to spring upon the bird and make a meal of him! But it would have been shameful to kill a creature who had come looking for help.

"There are those in this forest who would kill me and eat me," the bird said, making a sad face. "As you are my friends, I ask your protection."

"This is too much!" the fox cried. "You come to us for food and for shelter. Now you ask our protection. You know well who it is who wants to eat you, and you have made us powerless by trusting us."

Then the lion and the fox left the forest and went where they might hunt food more fairly.

"How did you force them to go?" the bird was asked by his friends.

"It is said, and truly," the bird replied, "that there is great strength in weakness."

"What a fine tale!" Nuri said, when it was done. "But certainly the bird deserved to be victorious.

"Such reward was not deserved by a certain fellow named Feraj. Please be silent while I acquaint you with his history."

Feraj and
the Magic Flute

THERE was once a small lute which stood in the hall of a beautiful house. The owners of the house had been poor, but when an uncle died, leaving the lute to them, their fortunes rose.

A sly fellow named Feraj guessed that the lute was the reason for the family's sudden wealth. Stealing the lute and carrying it into the desert, he tapped it and thumped it and pummeled it, finding nothing unusual about it. Exhausted from his wicked deed, he lay down to sleep, the lute on the ground beside him. The night wind sighed through the strings of the lute, crooning secrets of great wealth to be found, and rich rewards. Hearing none of this, Feraj slept.

For many days, Feraj kept the lute, examining it and

puzzling over it during the day and sleeping beside it at night while it sang out its stories.

At length he tired of the matter. Meeting a witless young man on a dusty road, he traded the lute to him for the cottage in which the young man and his mother lived. "It will surely make you rich," he told the young man, "for it has wondrous powers. I only trade it for reasons of health, that I may live in your simple cottage and regain my strength."

With that, he made such a poor face that the young man felt sorry for him and declared it a bargain.

"Dunce!" cried the young man's mother, when she learned what her son had done. "If the lute is magic, why then didn't it give the fellow a cottage?"

Having no answer for that, the luckless young man wailed pitifully.

At dawn of the following day, Feraj came to take possession of the cottage, driving the young man and his mother out. In her cloak the mother carried cold mutton and bread, while the young man dragged the lute sadly behind him. They had to go into the desert to live; there was no help for it. The young man howled, the mother wailed, and the day passed.

That night, awakening from the chill of the desert air, the young man heard a strange sound. Thinking his ears were playing tricks on him, he turned over and drew his cloak close about his head. The sound came again. Sitting up, the young man listened, and soon he discovered it was the lute that was making the noise.

"A bag of gold," it seemed to be repeating again and again, and "There, in the sand by your foot."

The young man rose quietly, thinking not to disturb his mother, and began to dig in the sand. At length his hands touched something solid and he soon unearthed a bag of gleaming gold.

The young man shook his mother rudely to waken her and showed her what he had found. Then the greedy old woman jiggled and joggled the lute, scolding it all the while, thinking to get even more gold. But, since dawn had come, the lute was silent.

"It was not the lute that told you, stupid fellow," cried the mother, "but some kind of dream." She tied the gold into the corner of her cloak. Then she and her son started for the city, planning what the money would buy.

In the city, they purchased fruit from a peddler's cart, gaped at the sights, and outfitted themselves in fine clothes and sandals of decorated leather.

Never had they looked so grand! As they strolled along the street, they were mistaken by the king's vizier for persons of noble position.

"May I be of service to you?" asked the vizier.

"We have recently left our home and are in need of a situation," the old woman told him.

Upon hearing this, the vizier prevailed upon them to travel to the region they had so recently left and there to reside in a magnificent house as overseers of the king's lands.

This they did gladly. Thirty servants were theirs, and forty rooms. And whom should they find employed at cleaning pots in the cooking chamber but Feraj! He had fallen asleep, leaving the cottage fire untended, and the home he had taken from them had burned to the ground.

Happy in the good fortune that had befallen them, the young man and his mother forgave Feraj completely for deceiving them about the lute. They even returned the lute to his hands, for the mother was convinced it was useless.

The rest of Feraj's long life was spent in service in the cooking chamber. Often he played fine airs upon the lute for the enjoyment of his fellow workers. But because he labored so hard during the daytime, he slept soundly all night, never hearing the night breezes in the lute strings, never learning the secret of the lute.

Nuri finished the story and leaned back, sighing.

"What do you think of that?" he inquired.

"I found it fascinating," the ogre admitted. "You know some very fine stories. I believe, however, that I have one that will outdo all of yours. It is a tale of magic and mystery. How fortunate you are that I am about to tell it to you."

The Rubies of Isfahan

IN former times, when reality was but a step from fairyland, there dwelled in the East a king who had a willful daughter called Fatima. So insistent was Fatima upon having her own way in all things that her father could deny her nothing. At last, however, she made a request that the king could not grant.

"Since I have passed all of my days inside the walls of this palace," she said one day, "I have made up my mind to travel with the next trade caravan that leaves here and see something of the world."

"Impossible!" her father cried. "These are dangerous times and caravans proceed only at great risk. Robbers camp along the roads, waiting for a chance to

pounce upon innocent travelers. I would not even
send caravans out were it not for the fact that the royal
rubies of Isfahan have disappeared, leaving us in
poverty."

"Nevertheless," Fatima declared, "I shall go with
the next caravan! I believe it leaves this very night."

"You shall not go!" the king declared firmly. Sum-
moning his vizier, the king commanded that Fatima be
locked in her apartment and kept there until the
caravan had departed from the palace.

But the willful princess, disguised as a camel boy,
lowered herself from the window of her apartment by
means of a knotted cord and took a place at the rear of
the line of march. There she remained for six days,
obeying the orders of the caravan master and doing her
best to keep pace with the rest of the company.

At last, one evening, weary from heat and travel, she
strolled from the place where her companions slept,
intending to enjoy the cool night air. But as she sat on a
hilly place, viewing the stars, fatigue overcame her
and she slept. While she slept, dawn came and the
caravan passed on, so that when she awoke she found
herself entirely alone.

She ran as far as she was able in the direction she felt
right, but could find no sign of the caravan, for shifting
sand had covered the tracks.

"What am I to do?" Fatima wailed. Throwing
herself down upon the ground, she wept bitterly. "I
am hopelessly lost and without food and water to keep
me alive."

But after she had lain that way for some time, pitying herself, her willful nature once more began to assert itself. "This will not do!" she said, rising and brushing the sand from her robe. "I must find a way out of this predicament."

She screwed up her face and thought hard, looking at the sun and trying to recall the method of telling direction by it. Then, choosing a route that seemed at least as good as any other, she set out across the sand. For hours she walked, straining her eyes to see signs of the caravan or of a village. At last night came, and thousands of stars glittered in the ink-black sky.

"I must rest!" Fatima thought. "I'm exhausted."

Settling herself upon the ground, she drew her robe close about her and tried to sleep. But before long she grew so cold that she had to rise and begin walking again to warm herself.

For hours she trudged, seeing nothing but the great round moon, countless stars, and the seemingly endless desert.

"Things could be no worse than this!" Fatima thought. "If only I had obeyed my father I would be safe in my own bed at this very moment."

But when the first faint light of dawn lit up the eastern sky, Fatima stopped short and rubbed her eyes in disbelief. There before her, like a pearl in the rosy glow of morning, lay the most beautiful city she had ever seen. There were small, neat houses, orchards of ripe fruit, and carefully tended gardens. In the center of all was a palace more lovely than the one Fatima

had so recently left. Its domes were patterned with gold and its towers were capped with gleaming silver.

"Here is help," Fatima cried joyously. "I am saved!"

She ran toward the city, falling from time to time in the soft sand but rising to laugh, brush herself off, and run again.

As she entered the city, Fatima noticed a coffee peddler sitting by the side of the street. "Ho!" Fatima cried. "I'm a stranger here and in need of help.

The coffee peddler stared at her. "That is your misfortune," he said, "for this is the city of Khadija, the sorceress queen. She helps no one."

"She cannot be as bad as that," Fatima said. "Who could refuse aid to a weary traveler?"

The coffee peddler made a sorrowful face. "Khadija could," he said. "My advice to you is to leave this place at once, before she discovers that you are here."

"That I cannot do," Fatima said, "for I am lost and don't know which way to go to reach my home. I will go to the palace and ask Khadija's help. Surely she will not turn me away."

The coffee peddler went away, shaking his head sadly, and Fatima proceeded to the palace.

Two guards intercepted her at the enormous iron gates and escorted her to the audience chamber where Khadija sat upon a gleaming gold throne.

Fatima approached the sorceress. "I have come to ask your help, oh queen of the age, queen without equal!" she said.

Khadija regarded Fatima thoughtfully for a long moment. "What is your name?" she asked at last, "and where do you come from?"

"I am the daughter of King Jaafar," Fatima told her. "My name is Fatima and I have become separated from my father's caravan."

Khadija leaped from her throne, her eyes shining with excitement. "This is wonderful news," she cried. "It is a stroke of good fortune!"

"Then you'll help me?" Fatima asked eagerly.

The queen smiled wickedly. "Quite the contrary," she said. "You are going to help me. For some time I have been seeking a means by which I could take control of your father's kingdom. Now fate has placed you in my hands."

"What are you going to do?" Fatima cried, shrinking back from the throne.

Khadija laughed.

"Why, hold you captive, of course," she said, "until your father pays a generous ransom . . . his entire kingdom. I'll send the ransom note at once."

Clapping her hands, Khadija summoned a servant and dictated a letter. Fatima listened with horror.

"Take the prisoner to the pomegranate garden," Khadija commanded the guards when the letter had been completed. "There she shall remain until her father agrees to my terms."

Fatima was conducted to a garden where fountains bubbled and roses twined. The entire garden was ringed with pomegranate trees.

"This will be your prison," one of the guards said.

"Prison?" Fatima echoed in surprise. "Why, there are no gates or locks! I could leave here any time I pleased."

"You will not find leaving an easy matter," the second guard said. "This is no ordinary garden."

Then the two guards fastened a thickly folded veil around Fatima's head, covering her eyes. In a moment the princess felt herself soaring through the air. Before she became accustomed to the sensation, she landed with a thump upon the ground.

"Untie the veil," one of the guards directed. His voice seemed far away.

Loosening the veil, Fatima was astonished to find herself standing inside the garden, while the two guards remained outside.

"I had forgotten that Queen Khadija is a sorceress," Fatima said.

"No one can match her magic," one of the guards assured her. "Here you will remain until she chooses to release you."

Then the guards departed, leaving Fatima to consider her plight.

"When I was lost in the desert," she thought, "I believed matters could be no worse. But since that time the situation has worsened considerably."

Sitting down at the edge of a fountain, she trailed her hand through the cool water. How, she wondered, could her lovely plan to see the world have turned out so badly? Somehow she must escape from the garden and from the city. Somehow she must return to her father's kingdom before he had to surrender it to Khadija.

Wrinkling her forehead, she thought hard.

"First," she decided, "I'll try to find a way through the pomegranate trees. Perhaps there is an opening that leads outside."

Going to the edge of the garden, she searched for an exit. But each time she found an opening between the thickly growing trees, she was pulled back into the garden as though by some unseen hand.

"Very well," Fatima said at last, "if I cannot go through, then I will go over." She selected one of the tallest trees, secured a foothold, and climbed upward. But no sooner did she reach the upper branches than she was flung down upon the ground. Picking herself up, she selected another tree and began climbing, only to be flung down once more.

"I am growing determined," Fatima muttered, feeling her old willful nature surging forth. The day had grown very hot, and she paused to mop her brow with a corner of her veil.

"If I cannot go through," she said, "and I cannot go over, then I will go under."

Then she stooped down and began scooping away the earth with her hands, preparing to make a tunnel. She had dug for only a few moments when she came upon a brass seal set in the ground. Lifting it with some effort, Fatima discovered a staircase leading to a deep cavern.

"Since matters can grow no worse," Fatima decided, "I may as well see what is down there."

She made her way down the staircase, stepping carefully, but when she had descended only a few steps, she found herself in darkness. Feeling her way along the wall, she moved on. At length she reached the bottom of the stairs. "If only I could see," Fatima thought, "I would know what to do next."

At that moment she reached out and felt before her an object that was smooth and cold. Kneeling down, she explored it with her hands. "I believe it is some sort of container," she decided, "and it seems to be full, for though it is covered with a lid, it is very heavy."

Taking the container in her arms, Fatima ascended the staircase slowly and carefully. When she reached the top she stepped out into the garden and set the heavy object down upon the ground. "It's a brass pot!" she said, lifting the lid. "I wonder what's inside."

Fatima drew in her breath sharply as the sunlight shone on the contents of the pot.

"Rubies!" she cried. "These are my father's rubies, I'm certain of it! They are the very ones that disappeared from his palace."

She knelt down, feeling the cool gems with the tips of her fingers. "Now I understand that it was Khadija who stole these, or at any rate they were stolen at her command. Doubtless she intended to reduce my father to a state of poverty so that he would be unable to maintain his kingdom. What a cruel queen she is!"

Suddenly Fatima was struck by a happy thought.

"I have caused a great deal of trouble by being disobedient," she said to herself. "I am truly sorry and will not make the same mistake again. But if I can escape from this place and return the rubies to my father, then I will be able to make up somewhat for the wrong I have done."

She sat down beside the pot to think. Somehow there must be a way out of the garden. "But how?" she wondered aloud.

"That is a very good question!" said a voice.

Fatima looked up in surprise. Above her, in the branches of a pomegranate tree, sat a large black crow.

Since so many strange things had occurred since her arrival in the garden, Fatima did not find it odd that a crow should address her.

"I was wondering," she told him, "how I can escape from this place and take with me these rubies, which are the property of my father, King Jaafar."

Then she told the crow how she had come to that place.

"I see," the crow said, when he had heard the story. Flying down, he took a closer look at the potful of gems. "Perhaps I can help you."

"You?" Fatima cried in surprise. "What could you do?"

"I too am a stranger here," the crow said, "attracted to the garden by the sight of the bubbling fountains. I cannot help but believe that two brains are better than

one. Together we will find a solution to your problem."

"Perhaps you are right," Fatima said. "I have not
done well by myself."

Rising, she went to the pomegranate trees and
demonstrated how she had tried to escape. As before,
she was pulled back into the garden by some invisible
force. Then, climbing one of the trees, she was flung to
the ground as she had been in her previous attempts to
escape.

"You see," she said, "it is hopeless."

The crow nodded. "So it seems," he said. "I cannot
help but wonder how you got in here to begin with."

"Oh," Fatima said, "that was the simplest of matters."

She described how the guards had blindfolded her
and how she had soared through the air. "As quickly as
could be, I found myself in the garden," she said.

"Where is the veil now?" the crow asked.

"Why, I don't know," Fatima said. "I suppose it's
here someplace. When I untied it, I simply let it fall to
the ground."

"Perhaps," the crow suggested, "it will take you out
of the garden as easily as it brought you in."

Whereupon the two rushed about, searching beside
the fountains and beneath the rose bushes for the
missing veil.

"I've found it!" Fatima cried, holding up the blue
veil for the crow to see.

"Splendid," the crow said. "Now let us go back for the gems."

Through the garden they hurried, to the spot where they had left the rubies.

"Place the veil around your head," the crow ordered, "and I will tie the ends with my beak."

With the veil over her eyes, Fatima felt the crow take hold of the ends and loop them securely. "Now, pick up the pot," the crow prompted. "Then we shall see what will happen."

No sooner had Fatima grasped the pot than she felt herself leave the ground and soar upward. In another moment she landed with a thump.

The crow was cawing excitedly. "You've done it!" he shrieked. "I followed you straight out over the trees."

When he loosened the veil from Fatima's eyes, she saw that she was once again outside the garden. The crow flapped happily about.

"Your problem has been solved," he cried gleefully.

Fatima sat down upon the pot of rubies, her chin in her hands. "Half of my problem has been solved," she said.

"I don't understand," the crow said. "You are out of the garden. Now you have only to return to your father, bearing the royal rubies."

"My dear friend," Fatima said, "fly to the tallest branch of the tree in which you are sitting and tell me what you see."

The crow did as Fatima bade him. "I see the city,"

he said, shading his eyes with one wing, "and beyond it, the desert."

"Exactly," Fatima said sadly. "I have escaped from the garden, but I have not escaped from the city. And if I do manage to escape from the city, how will I find my way across that desert to my home?"

The crow scratched the top of his head thoughtfully. "This is more complicated than I realized," he said, "but all is not lost. Conceal yourself here in the lilac bushes and I will fly to the palace. You would be astonished to learn how many bits of useful information birds hear at open windows. I may be able to learn in which direction your father's kingdom lies."

So saying, he spread his wings and flew off toward the palace.

Fatima set the potful of rubies in the lilac bushes and concealed herself as best she could to await the crow's return. In nearly no time he was back, his black eyes dancing with excitement.

"I have news!" he cried. "Queen Khadija did not dispatch the ransom note to your father as she had intended. Instead, she has decided to go to him herself, announce the news of your capture, and demand his kingdom."

Fatima frowned.

"I don't see why you are so excited about that bit of news," she said. "The end of the matter will be the same."

"You don't understand," the crow said impatiently. "At this moment the queen's caravan is being prepared. She will travel over the desert in great comfort."

"I still don't see—" Fatima began.

"You will," said the crow. "Since you are expert at hiding away on caravans, you can conceal yourself in this one. Then, when the caravan reaches your father's palace, the queen will be furious to learn that she has transported you, as well as the royal rubies, to your very doorstep."

"Oh," Fatima cried, jumping up and down, "that is a splendid trick! I will go at once and slip into the caravan."

Locating the caravan, Fatima crept in amidst the baggage and settled down, cradling the potful of rubies on her lap.

"The queen is coming," the crow cawed, darting down to where Fatima hid. "Are you ready to go?"

"Ready and anxious!" Fatima whispered. "I have seen all of the wide world I care to see."

For many days the caravan traveled, passing through the trackless desert. Fatima dined upon apples which she had tucked into the folds of her robe before leaving the city. She had water too, from a flask the crow had thoughtfully provided.

Sometimes at night, when the caravan had halted and all the company was asleep, Fatima slipped from the huge pile of baggage to breathe the clear desert air. The crow would fly down from his perch atop the baggage, and the two would have a pleasant chat.

At length the caravan reached its destination. Through the broad street of the great city and straight to the royal palace it went, attracting curious crowds.

"I have come to speak with King Jaafar," Khadija called to the guards at the gate. "Tell him to come to me at once."

Hastening up the steps, the guards returned with Jaafar.

"The time has come to surprise Queen Khadija," the crow hissed.

"I am ready," Fatima whispered, preparing to climb down from the pile of baggage.

"I have news of your daughter, the Princess Fatima," Khadija announced.

"Tell me quickly!" the king cried. "I have been desolate since her disappearance."

"Here I am, Father!" Fatima called, jumping down from her hiding place. "Queen Khadija held me captive and she came here to demand your kingdom in payment for my return."

"What is this you say?" the king demanded, running to his daughter.

"That is not all," Fatima continued. "In this pot are your rubies, which I discovered in a cavern beneath Queen Khadija's garden."

The crow cawed happily, darting from Fatima to Queen Khadija and back again.

"What say you to all this?" the king demanded, turning to Khadija.

Realizing that because of Fatima's escape she herself no longer had the advantage, Khadija hastened to conceal what she had done.

"I am at a loss to explain it," she cried. "Your daughter came to seek my aid, and at great expense I fitted out this caravan in order to transport her safely home. I do not understand why she should turn on me, making such outrageous charges."

"That is not true," Fatima declared. "I can prove my story. Lift the lid of the pot and see the rubies of Isfahan for yourself."

The king lifted the lid.

"Olives!" he cried. "I do not understand this at all."

"I am beginning to understand," Fatima said. "I had forgotten that Queen Khadija is a sorceress. I'm sure she transformed the rubies into olives!"

"You cannot prove that!" Khadija snapped.

"Perhaps I can," the crow said.

Flying to his perch atop the baggage, he returned with a large, glistening ruby, which he placed in the king's hand.

"Because of my fondness for shiny objects," he said, "I removed that ruby from the pot and kept it beside me throughout the journey. I intended to replace it as soon as Khadija had been found out."

Clapping his hands together, the king summoned his vizier and instructed him to inspect the potful of olives.

"These are not ordinary olives," the vizier said when he had completed his examination. "They have not come across the desert in this pot, for they appear to be very fresh. It is my opinion that they are not truly olives at all, but objects cast over by an enchantment."

"Can you remove the enchantment?" the king inquired.

"I can," the vizier replied. "But if I do, then all the magic powers will be taken from the person who cast the enchantment."

"Don't do it!" Khadija wailed.

But the king raised his hand for silence. "Let it be done!" he commanded.

The vizier spun quickly on his heels and recited a strange rhyme. In less than a minute the olives had become glistening rubies once more.

"What will I do without my magic powers?" Khadija moaned.

"You will return to your own land and rule it wisely," King Jaafar said. "Begone!"

Khadija climbed gloomily upon her camel and signaled for the caravan to depart.

Fatima, content thenceforth to remain in her father's kingdom, spent long, blissful hours strolling through the royal gardens in the company of her faithful friend the clever crow.

"Oh" Nuri cried, "if only I could rely upon crows or magic to solve my problem with you! Unfortunately, I have only my wits, and I must do with them the best that I can, as did the young man called Zeki, some time ago."

"You will tell me about him, of course," the ogre said.

"Of course," Nuri replied.

Zeki the Witless

IN days gone by, when anything could happen, and often did, there lived in the East a widow who had one son, Zeki. It was Zeki's duty to walk each day through the streets of the town, selling bread from his mother's oven. But though Zeki was an industrious young man and did his best with the task at hand, business did not flourish.

"It has come to my attention," he said to his mother one day, "that there is no food in our house."

"That is unfortunately true," his mother replied. "There is not even money enough for purchasing flour, and so I can bake no more bread for sale. Someone must gather the rugs from the floor and transport them to the city. There they may fetch a good price and we will be able to eat once again."

"That is a splendid idea!" Zeki cried enthusiastically. "When you have sold the rugs, please purchase a bit of sugar candy, since I have a sudden craving for sweets."

"Dunce!" his mother snapped. "An old woman cannot carry rugs to the city and peddle them. You will need to go. My only regret is that you are so witless. You will probably wander off into the sunset and never be heard from again. But go you must, and there is no help for it."

Gathering up three small carpets from the floor and thrusting them into Zeki's outstretched arms, the widow led her son from the house and set him upon the road, pointing him in the proper direction.

Following his nose down the road, Zeki traveled through valleys and over rolling hills to the great city. He entered the gates anxious to see all there was to see. "If I finish my work quickly," he decided, "I will have some time to view the sights."

With that, he took the carpets from beneath his arm, unrolled them, and spread them out at his feet.

"Rugs!" he called out. "I have rugs for sale."

Passersby stared at him, then hurried on. An old man laughed rudely.

"See here," cried a black-robed man, rushing up to Zeki, "you cannot sell your rugs here. There is a law that forbids the conducting of such business anywhere but in the bazaar."

"Oh," Zeki mumbled, embarrassed at having made such a mistake. "I didn't know, for I am from the country and only a dunce at that. Would you kindly direct me to the bazaar?".

Pointing a long finger, the black-robed man indicated the direction in which Zeki must go. Zeki, anxious to leave the place where he had shown himself to be a fool, rolled up his rugs and set off down the street.

The great bazaar was like a city in itself. It was immense and covered completely by a roof. A deafening clamor sounded from within.

Entering a gate, Zeki followed one of the narrow streets that wound through the bazaar. All around were stalls displaying goods. There were fruits, from raisins to huge melons, brass pots shining in the sunlight, and all manner of clothing.

At length Zeki came to a stall where two men sat sipping coffee. Before them was a brightly patterned carpet, and in a tall pile behind them there were many more carpets. One of the men was small and neatly dressed while the other, an enormous, black-bearded man, wore flashing gold rings in his ears and a turban of green silk upon his head. Zeki could hear their conversation clearly from where he stood.

"If you were to sell this rug," the smaller man said, "what price would you ask for it?"

"Ah," the huge man groaned, "may I be struck by misfortune if ever I should sell this rug, the masterpiece of my collection!"

"So that is how it is done," Zeki thought. "Such remarks on the part of the seller will only serve to make the buyer more anxious, thereby causing the price to rise. I am such a dunce that I never would have thought of the scheme, but I believe I can do it, if only I can find a place to display my rugs. They are certainly finer than any rugs in that fellow's stall."

Beside the stall of the bearded man was a tiny vacant nook. Zeki unrolled his rugs and knelt to arrange them there.

"What are you doing?" A booming voice demanded. Looking up, Zeki saw the black-bearded man standing over him. His arms were folded across his chest and his face wore an angry expression.

"Why," Zeki answered, "I am preparing to sell these rugs."

"You will not sell them here," the huge man bellowed. "I am the only rug dealer in this bazaar."

"Perhaps you were until today," Zeki said, "but now I am here."

"I don't think you understand," the man said, his voice becoming oily. "I am called Kerim the Cunning. When I arrived in this city, there were many rug dealers here. But all of that has changed. I persuaded the other dealers to go elsewhere and to leave the bazaar to me." He smiled a wicked smile. "Will it be necessary for me to persuade you to leave?"

"But I cannot sell my rugs outside the bazaar," Zeki protested, "for such commerce is forbidden."

"Then I suggest you go to another city," Kerim the Cunning said.

Zeki shook his head vigorously. "That I cannot do," he said. "My poor widowed mother waits at home for me to bring the proceeds from the rugs. She has not a mouthful of food to eat, and at this very moment she may be starving to death."

"What a pity," Kerim said, pretending to wipe a tear from his eye. "My heart goes out to her. I urge you to hurry to another city and sell those rugs as quickly as you can."

Zeki stared at him in disbelief.

"Surely you will let me sell my rugs here, now that you have heard my story," he said.

Kerim the Cunning tugged thoughtfully at his black beard. "Look at it this way," he said. "If three people purchase rugs from you, then those are three customers I have lost. You would be taking bread from my mouth, and I cannot allow that to happen."

He advanced toward Zeki, scowling fiercely. "I have wasted too much time on you already," he bellowed. "Pick up those rugs and leave here at once!"

Terrified, Zeki snatched up the rugs and ran stumbling down the road toward the gate. Twice he fell and needed to pick himself up.

"Oh, what will I do now?" he wailed, when he stood once more outside the bazaar. "I cannot sell the rugs outside the bazaar and I cannot sell them inside."

He sat down in the street, the rugs across his lap and

his chin in his hands. "If only I were not such a dunce," he thought gloomily, "I might think of a solution to the problem."

Traffic streamed by Zeki. There were donkeys laden with produce from the country and city folk scurrying about. At any other time, Zeki would have watched the comings and goings with delight, but now he paid no attention to his surroundings. His mind wrestled with the problem at hand.

Through the day, Zeki sat thus, struggling with the knotty puzzle. At last the sun sank below the western horizon and a chilly wind blew, ruffling Zeki's robe.

The great iron gates of the bazaar were swung shut and locked.

"Kerim the Cunning must be sleeping now," Zeki sighed. "No doubt he fell asleep while counting the proceeds from his day's business." Zeki yawned. "I too am tired," he thought, "but I must be up early in the morning if I am to outwit Kerim the Cunning."

Then he gave a little squeal of joy. "That's it," he cried. "I'll scale the wall, make my way to the rug market, and sell my rugs before Kerim the Cunning awakens!"

Zeki leaped to his feet, tucked the rugs beneath his arm once more, and hurried to the bazaar. The streets were deserted. Overhead, a full moon shone, bathing the city in silvery light. Gripping the rugs tightly, Zeki took a little running jump and began his ascent up a tall tree that stood beside the wall of the bazaar. After much struggling he reached the top. There he sat for a moment, surveying the bazaar. How lovely it looked in the moonlight, its stalls and twisting streets like a frosted fairyland.

"Here I go," he whispered, dropping from the wall and landing with a thud upon the ground below. He took the rugs from beneath his cloak and started down the winding street toward the cloth market, moving quietly lest he should awaken some merchant and be questioned about his strange behavior.

When he reached the stall of Kerim the Cunning, Zeki paused for a moment and then tiptoed past it, holding his breath.

He spread the rugs in the tiny nook beside Kerim's stall and sat down upon them. How tired he was. He had not slept since arriving in the city

"I will stretch out here on the carpets," he decided. "I will not sleep, but only rest a little. When the dawn breeze blows I will arise and prepare for the opening of the gates. Surely Kerim the Cunning does not arise that early."

He lay down on the rugs and closed his eyes. The wool was soft beneath his head, and he felt himself drifting into a land of deep cushions and scented down.

Gradually Zeki became aware of sounds around him. Sunlight shone through his closed eyelids.

"Well, well!" a voice above him boomed, "what have we here?"

Zeki cautiously opened one eye, then the other, and saw the sight he had feared. Kerim the Cunning stood over him, a scowl on his face. Zeki had slept, and while he slept, daylight had come. Crowds of shoppers filled the streets.

"I only thought—" Zeki began, rising from the carpets.

"You thought to be here before I awoke," Kerim roared, "but I have found you out! Now pick up those rugs and leave here, so that I may go about my business."

He shook his fist menacingly at Zeki, and his black eyes gleamed.

"I'm going," Zeki assured him, snatching up his rugs. He trotted off down the street, glancing over his shoulder from time to time to see Kerim the Cunning, his golden earrings glistening in the sunlight, standing before his stall.

Once outside the bazaar, Zeki sat down to consider matters. His plan had failed; his effort had been in vain.

"At least I had a good night's sleep," he thought, seeing the bright side. "Now I am rested. If only I were not so stupid, I would devise some clever scheme for getting inside that bazaar. Poor mother must be growing very hungry!"

At the thought of food, Zeki groaned. Closing his eyes, he envisioned mutton and plump raisins simmering in butter. Opening his eyes, he glanced about.

Surely in a city of such abundance there was a fig or a date for a country boy. His eyes lit upon a heavily laden donkey being driven down the street by a farmer.

Zeki was struck by an idea. That farmer might provide him with both breakfast and a means of gaining entrance to the bazaar. Zeki had observed that the fruit stalls were located next to the cloth market. If he, Zeki, could slip unnoticed into the fruit stalls, perhaps he could show his rugs without being seen by Kerim the Cunning. It was worth a try. Quickly he concealed the rugs beneath his cloak.

"Ho," Zeki cried, hailing the farmer. "I wish to strike a bargain with you."

The farmer regarded Zeki suspiciously. "What do you want?" he demanded.

"I will accompany you into the bazaar and assist you in the sale of your wares," Zeki told him. "All you need pay me is a piece of fruit. What say you?"

The farmer considered for a moment, then motioned for Zeki to help himself to an apple.

"Take two," the farmer said generously. "You cannot work with an empty stomach."

Zeki munched hungrily upon the apples. Then, falling in line behind the farmer and his donkey, he entered the bazaar once more. Down the dusty street they went, past stalls, past haggling shoppers and merchants.

"We will stop here," the farmer said, as they reached

the fruit market. Directly past the farmer's head, Zeki could see Kerim the Cunning, his green turban sitting squarely atop his head.

"I will stand on the far side of the donkey," Zeki said, "and offer the apples for sale."

"That is a very good idea," the farmer observed. "I will stay on this side. We will not even need to unload the donkey."

Whereupon he began to cry his wares and Zeki, going around to the other side of the donkey, did likewise.

Before long, Zeki grew bold and took from beneath his cloak the rugs, which he proceeded to describe for potential buyers. He was close to making a sale when the farmer, seeing what Zeki was about, cried out in alarm.

"You cannot sell rugs in the fruit market," he said. "Such a thing is unlawful and I will not be a party to it!"

"Who sells rugs in the fruit market?" a familiar voice roared.

Through the crowd that had gathered came Kerim the Cunning.

"You!" he thundered. "Out! Out!"

Zeki clutched the rugs to him, turned and dashed off down the street. Taking apples from the donkey's pack, Kerim the Cunning pelted the retreating Zeki with them.

Panting, Zeki reached the gate and the safety that lay

beyond it. "Oh, what shall I do?" he wailed, mopping his brow with a corner of his cloak. "If only I were clever." He sighed and shook his head sadly.

"If I were clever," he continued, "then I would manage to gain entrance to the bazaar and stay until I had sold the rugs. What a pity mother did not come. Kerim the Cunning would not dare to drive out an old woman."

Zeki leaped up, struck by a sudden inspiration.

"That's it!" he cried. "I'll disguise myself as an old woman. Then Kerim the Cunning will not threaten me."

Among the passersby were several women who carried bundles of freshly laundered clothing. Waiting until he saw one of his own size, one with kindly eyes, Zeki approached her.

"I could weave some unlikely tale to explain why I must borrow some of your laundry," he told her, "but I am a truthful fellow. I throw myself upon your mercy." So saying, he told the old woman the story of his journey to the city, of his poor hungry mother, and of Kerim the Cunning.

The old woman wept many tears of sympathy at so tragic a tale, then outfitted Zeki with clothing from her bundle. "I will wait here until you have sold your rugs," she told him. "Good fortune to you."

Zeki marched resolutely through the bazaar gate once again, confident that he had outwitted Kerim the Cunning at last.

Straight to the cloth market he went, then spread his rugs once again in the nook beside Kerim's stall.

"What does this mean?" Kerim the Cunning demanded.

"I am only a poor old woman," Zeki croaked. "Surely there is space here for me to sell my simple little carpets."

Kerim the Cunning circled Zeki suspiciously.

"There is something familiar about you," he said, tugging at his beard. "Have we met before?"

Zeki shook his head vigorously.

"I am certain we haven't," he croaked.

"There is also something familiar about your rugs," Kerim continued. He stopped suddenly and stared at Zeki's slippers, the one part of his costume that had remained unchanged. A light dawned in Kerim's eyes.

"You!" he screeched. "It's you again!" With that, he gave the unfortunate Zeki a clout upon the head.

Zeki seized his rugs and fled, veils flying.

"Should you return, you will regret it," Kerim shouted after him.

"Once more I have been defeated," Zeki moaned, reaching the safety of the city streets. When he had returned the borrowed articles of clothing to their rightful owner and thanked her for her kindness, the miserable young man sat down to think.

"It's no use," he decided sadly. "I am no match for Kerim the Cunning. But I am surprised that such an unfair practice can continue in the city of the sultan himself. If only I were not such a dunce, I would go to the sultan and tell him what is happening in the bazaar."

Zeki whooped with delight. "That is the very thing!" he cried happily. "If the sultan knew of Kerim the Cunning's unfairness, he would put a stop to it. And if I cannot go to the sultan, then the sultan must come here."

Gazing up the street to where the royal palace stood, Zeki smiled.

"I wonder how long it would take for a rumor to reach that palace," he thought. "Not long, I would guess."

Stopping a peddler who was going past, Zeki whispered in his ear. "Trouble in the bazaar!" he hissed.

The peddler's eyes grew wide. Hurrying on, he passed the word to a tradesman, then to a coffee peddler.

Zeki watched with satisfaction. Soon the street was buzzing with the news.

"Now," Zeki said, putting his rugs beneath his arm, "it is time I went into the bazaar to conduct my business." In only a few minutes, he had reached the cloth market and had spread his rugs out once more in the tiny nook.

"I cannot believe my eyes!" Kerim the Cunning screeched. "It cannot be you!"

"But it is," Zeki chirped. "I have come to sell my rugs."

Kerim clapped a hand to his forehead in exasperation. "You are not a very smart fellow," he complained.

"Oh, you are right," Zeki admitted brightly. "I'm really quite a dunce."

"Well, dunce," Kerim bellowed, "this is the last time you will bother me!" Whereupon he seized Zeki by the collar and shook him roughly.

So intent upon the business was Kerim the Cunning that he failed to notice the silence that had fallen upon the bazaar.

"What is the trouble here?" a stern voice at Kerim's shoulder demanded.

It was then that Kerim turned and saw beside him the sultan himself.

"It is nothing—nothing at all!" Kerim spluttered. "It is but a trifling matter and not worth your royal attention."

"I will be the judge of that," the sultan said. "Tell me your story," he continued, turning to Zeki.

Zeki related the story of his attempts to sell his rugs and of the hungry mother who awaited him.

When the sultan had heard the story, he declared that henceforth his viziers would oversee the bazaar, making sure that unfair practices did not exist. As for Kerim the Cunning, he was severely rebuked and warned to mend his ways.

"While you were speaking, I noticed the rugs at your feet," the sultan told Zeki. "They are three of the finest carpets I have ever seen. How did they come into your possession?"

"Oh, sir," Zeki said, "my mother fashioned them

with her own hands. They have lain in our home these many years."

"Does your mother still weave carpets?" the sultan inquired.

"Alas, no," Zeki said. "Our sheep died and we have no money for purchasing more."

"Such talent as your mother's must not be wasted!" the sultan said. "I will purchase these three rugs and place them in the palace. In addition to that, I will provide you with a flock of the finest sheep, so that your mother may produce more rugs. I will buy all that she can weave. What do you say to that?"

Zeki could scarcely believe his ears. He thanked the sultan again and again, dancing up and down in excitement.

"It is my guess," the sultan said, smiling, "that it was you who started the rumor of trouble at the bazaar so that I would come here. If that is so, then you are a clever young man."

Zeki was nearly overcome with joy. Was it possible that the sultan spoke the truth?

That evening, when the sun had sunk behind the western hills, Zeki started down the dusty road toward home. Gold jingled in his pouch, a bundle of delicacies swung from his shoulder, and a fine flock of sheep ambled before him. How anxious he was to tell his mother of the sultan's generosity, and also the very good news that he, Zeki, was not a dunce after all, but a clever young man.

"You too are a clever young man," the ogre told Nuri, "but I am not greedy and wicked as was Kerim the Cunning. In truth I am the gentlest and kindest of ogres."

"Prove it!" Nuri cried, filled with sudden inspiration.

"How?" the ogre asked suspiciously. "I am only kind and gentle when my heart has been touched. While you have entertained me with your stories, you have not touched my heart."

"It remains for another to do that," Nuri said, leaping to his feet and dashing into the merchant's house.

In only a moment he returned, bringing with him Lalla.

"See here!" Ox-Foot demanded. "What does this mean?"

"It means that my last and best strategy in gaining possession of the gold is to present Lalla to you and to force you to listen to her entreaties."

"I will not be swayed," Ox-Foot declared firmly.

"Please," Lalla cried, her great eyes filling with tears.

"Never," the ogre said, his voice breaking.

The tears spilled from Lalla's eyes and rolled down her cheeks.

"Stop that," Ox-Foot roared. "You are taking advantage of my soft heart!"

"Give me the gold," Nuri suggested, "and you shall

have a home in this garden for the remainder of your life. We will care for you and lavish love upon you. What say you?"

"Take the gold," Ox-Foot cried, "and welcome to it. Only make her stop weeping!"

Nuri took the gold from Ox-Foot and went to present it to the merchant. Then Lalla became Nuri's bride, and joy reigned.

For the remainder of his long life, Ox-Foot dwelt in great happiness with Nuri and Lalla, and when the time came for the ogre to withdraw behind the veil of mystery, he continued to rain blessings down upon his two friends and all of their descendants.